POLICE PURSUIT!

By Meredith Rusu
Illustrated by Paul Lee

SCHOLASTIC INC.

ISBN 978-1-338-11750-9

10 9 8 7 6 5 4   18 19 20 21
                                                                        40

Printed in the U.S.A
First printing 2017
Book design by Angela Jun

It is a beautiful morning in LEGO® City. The sun is shining. The birds are chirping. The crook is stealing money from the bank . . . Wait—what?!

"Heh, heh, heh." The crook laughs. "There's nothing like the smell of fresh money to go with my morning coffee."

Suddenly, the crook hears footsteps.
"Rats!" he says. "Looks like my coffee break is over—time to make my getaway!"

Outside, two police officers are on patrol.
An alert comes on their radio. A crook has just robbed the bank!

"Hey—do you see what I see?" the policeman asks. "Is that . . . money flying out of that car?"

"Pull over!" the policewoman shouts to the crook.

"Never!" cries the crook. He speeds away.

The police officers chase the crook all over LEGO City!

They drive over the river. "Boy, the fish are really biting today," says a fisherman.

They drive through the woods. "Look, Daddy! I thought you said money doesn't grow on trees?" says a boy.

They even drive past Grandmother's house. "Slow down, you whippersnappers!" yells Grandma.

Just when the crook thinks he's gotten away . . .
His tire blows out!

"Rats! Looks like it's onto plan *P*,"
the crook says. "Hiding in the *park*!"

But the police are hot on the crook's trail. The crook thinks fast and looks around the park for a way to disguise himself.

"Excuse us, sir. Have you seen this crook?" the policewoman asks.

"What's that now, deary? Have I seen your book? I'm afraid not," says the crook.

It looks like the police have fallen for his trick and they walk away. But then the police look back in the crook's direction, and back down at the photo. They might be on to him—he must find another disguise!

Looks like the hot dog vendor is taking a break . . .

"All this chasing is making me hungry. One hot dog, please," the policeman says. "Hey, do I know you?"

"Uh . . . no, sorry!" says the crook. Thinking fast, he squirts ketchup at the policeman and makes a run for it.

The crook finds a third disguise and hides by a man with a dog.
But the dog starts barking at him!

"That's odd," says the dog's owner. "Buster usually likes strangers."

Meanwhile, the police are walking their way. The crook runs off before the barking can attract attention.

"That was close," the crook says to himself. "I know! I'll blend in on the playground. The cops won't suspect that!"

"Let's go FASTER!" shouts one of the kids.
"What?" asks the crook. "*Whoaaaaaaaa!*"

Money goes flying from the crook's bag!
"Muh-ney! Muh-ney!" cries a baby.
"Oh, my, her first word!" cheers the baby's mother.

The crook gasps. If the baby doesn't keep quiet, the police will look his way!

"Shush kid," hisses the crook. "And I'll buy you a lollipop."

The police officers hear the baby crying and spot the crook nearby.

"Rats," groans the crook as they handcuff him. "I would have gotten away if it wasn't for that baby."

"There's no use crying over spilled milk," says the policeman. "Spilled money, perhaps."

"Your baby saved the day!" the policewoman tells the mother.

"That crook was clever," says the policeman. "But not clever enough to outsmart the city's youngest police officer in training."